2 427167 21

D0491587

We hope that you enjoy this Early Soundplay story again, and again, and again!

Children love repetition. It helps them build their knowledge and understanding of word meanings and story structure. Children also love sound play – it's fun! And it helps develop their ability to recognise and say speech sounds in different words. These are key foundation skills for success in phonics, early reading and spelling.

This story is full of sound play with a special focus on 's' and 's' blends. The simple, interactive storyline makes it easy for children to anticipate what happens next and to join in when they hear the story again. This provides lots of opportunities for them to both hear and practise saying 's' and 's' blend words.

Reading stories and looking at picture books together is one of the best ways in which you can support children's spoken and written language development.

Clickety Books Ltd
Victoria Beacon Place, Roche, Cornwall PL26 8LG, UK

All rights reserved. No part of this publication may be
reproduced, stored in a retrieval system, or transmitted, in
any form, or by any means, without the prior permission of
Clickety Books Ltd.

Illustrations ©Clickety Books Ltd 2015
Text ©Clickety Books Ltd 2015

First published by Clickety Books Ltd 2015

ISBN 978-1-907968-33-4

Printed and bound by Short Run Press Ltd
Exeter EX2 7LW, UK

www.clicketybooks.co.uk

RENFREWSHIRE COUNCIL	
242716721	
Bertrams	23/08/2017
	£6.99
REN	

Tess and Bess
in the Snow

Written by Sally Bates

Illustrated by Sarah-Leigh Wills

Series Editor Anne Ayre

Some things to look out for...

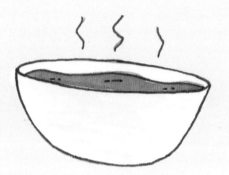

soup

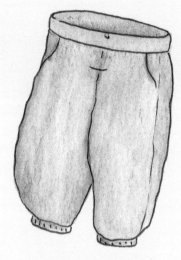

trousers

dress

boots

socks

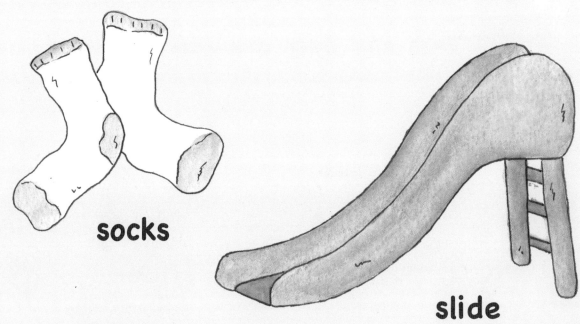

slide

cheesecake

jumper

Tess and Bess are VERY excited!

It is snowing
and the garden is sparkling white!

Tess and Bess get dressed:
pants, socks and vest,

trousers

woolly
jumper

dress

stripy scarf for Tess

spotty
scarf for
Bess.

Tess and Bess skip
down the steps, and
pull on their boots.

Ready steady off they go,
for a day full of fun in the snow!

Tess and Bess draw in the snow with sticks,

criss-cross
lines

squares

and
squiggles.

The little mice laugh and
squeak and giggle.

Tess and Bess put on their skates,
they slip and slide and glide across the ice!

They dance and
spin in circles

round and round!

Tess and Bess
jump on the sledge.
Whoosh! Off they go!

Faster, faster
across the snow,
faster and faster
down the hill

faster and faster,
until... until...

Oh no! The sledge hits a stone
and Tess and Bess
carry-on on their own!
See them fly, high in the sky.

And SPLAT in the snow,
deep and soft down below.

Tess and Bess turn somersaults in the snow,

over and over and over they go!

The little mice squeak and squeal with delight,
"Look at us! Look at us! We're all covered in white!"

Tess and Bess scamper back to the house.
Tess says to Bess "Let's make a snow-mouse!"

The snow-mouse is tall
with a long stripy tail,
two small stones for eyes
and a nose that's...
a snail!

Tess and Bess scoop snow into a ball,
throw it up in the air and watch it fall.

They throw another ball.
It hits the house
SPLAT against the wall!
Whoops!

And just misses Mummy mouse!

Tess and Bess sip hot soup,
and, for a treat,
a slice of cheesecake,
sticky and sweet.

Then a cuddle with Mummy mouse,
a story and bed!

Shh! Tess and Bess are fast asleep.
They are dreaming of snow thick and deep,

of sledging

and snowballs

and dancing on ice.

Sleep tight, little mice, sweet dreams and Good Night.

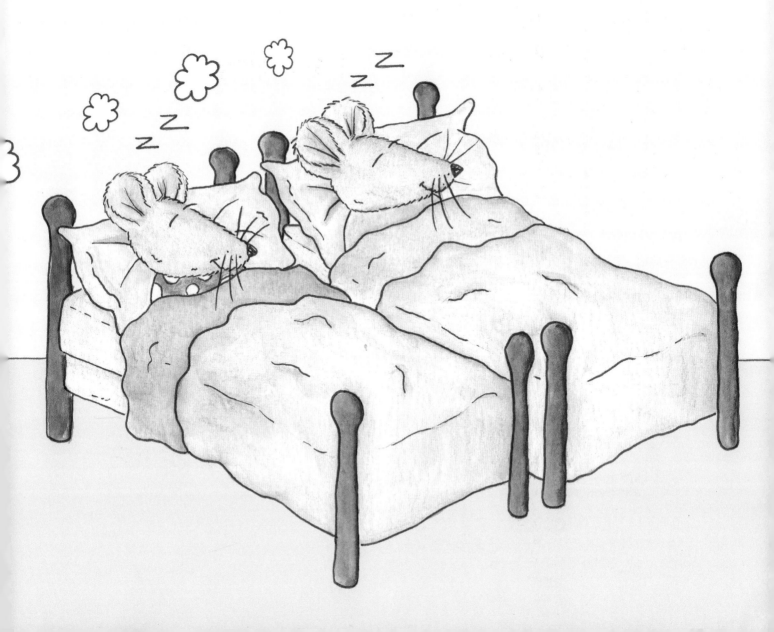

Did you spot Tess and Bess's special 's' blend words?

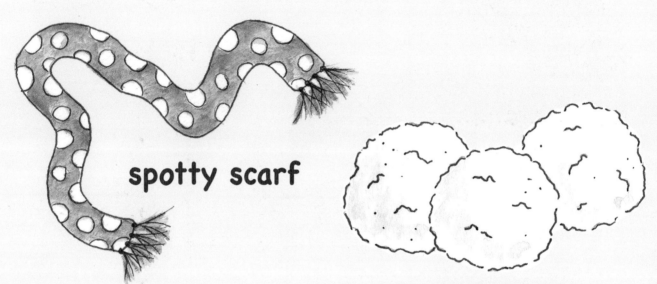

spotty scarf

snowballs

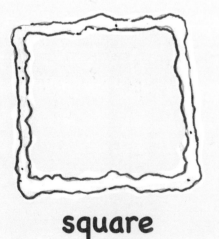

square

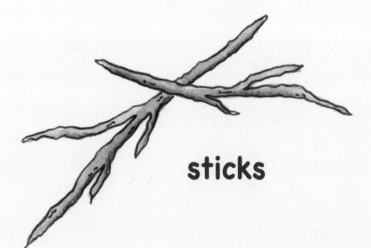

sticks

small stones

squiggles

sledge

stripy scarf

skates

More fun with Early Soundplay...

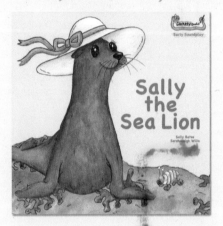

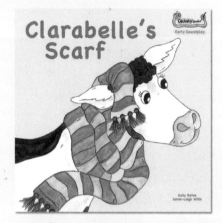

Look! Sally the Sea Lion is playing hide and seek on the beach with her best friend Ryan. Sally can't see Ryan anywhere. Can you see him?

Join Tess and Bess as they squeak and squeal having lots of fun in the snow! They go skating, sledging, snowballing and make a big snow-mouse.

It's cold on the cliffs. Clarabelle the calf has lost her scarf. She shivers and sniffs then giggles and laughs when she sees who's taken her scarf.

Chatty Bat loves to chitter chatter chat with everyone. It's very noisy with constant chatter until it's time to sleep - then no more chatter, not a peep!

Join Clip Clop and her friends Hip Hop the bunny, Yip Yap the puppy and Flip Flap the bird as they set off for a picnic. Clip clop, clippety clop.

Jake the snake likes baking cakes. Yummy scrummy cakes! However, he is a bit of a silly snake and ends up with a tummy ache.